The Eulogizer

Flairs and Glairs

Publication House

"The Eulogizer"

ISBN No: " 978-93-91302-28-3"
1st Edition
Language – English and Hindi

Flairs and Glairs
Publication House
Regd. Under MSME Act.

Disclaimer

This is a work of fiction and solely represent the thoughts of the corresponding authors of the articles. Our editors have tried their best to edit the content of all the authors and check the plagiarism.
All the write-ups in this book are unique and are only published in this book.
In case any plagiarism or error is found, only the author is responsible alone, and not the publisher or the Compilers.

Cover Designing and Book Formatting
Shubham Shah and Ishani Agarwal

Acknowledgement

We would like to express our special thanks and gratitude to all our co-authors and team members who helped us to publish this beautiful anthology. Without their hard-work, love and support, it would not be possible to publish our anthology.

We like to express our deepest thanks to Flairs and Glairs Publication, without whom this project would never been possible. We are thankful to the founder for giving us an opportunity to become successful compilers.

Moreover, a special thanks to our beloved parents, friends and well-wishers for their unconditional support and encouragement towards completing our anthology.

Finally, we wish to express our profound gratitude towards our Project Head, Muskan Shah for her guidance and support to complete our book without any hindrance.

Once again, we are thankful to everyone who helps us to complete this book with perfection, especially the co-authors, who are the key notes of this beautiful anthology.

Introduction

"THE EULOGIZER" exudes the theme 'The Person You Admire'. Life is full of surprises and we always expect to see someone more surprising and alluring.

People are everywhere yet we are captivated by certain someone. Sometimes, we are influenced by their actions unconsciously. They may be one of our families, a friend, a teacher, a celebrity, a leader or even may be a stranger. We like them particularly for their uniqueness. Yet we never had a chance to tell them or to express how we feel about them till now.

"THE EULOGIZER" is a family of more than fifty writers where the writers have revealed their unspoken feelings to the person they admire through their penning.

And we also hope the readers can find their unspoken feelings for the person they admire by reading through the pages of our beauteous anthology.

Co Authors

1. Shubham Shah (Publisher)
2. Muskan Shah (Project Head)
3. Subananthini. R (Compiler)
4. Christy Gnana Deepa (Co-Compiler)
5. Muthuselvi. R
6. Divyadharshini. R
7. Vasantha Ranjani. R
8. Umamaheshwari. K
9. Charulatha. V
10. Misbah Ismail
11. Sathish Balakumaran. S.N.I
12. Lakxana. S
13. Hemalatha. M
14. Priyanka. R
15. Tharani. U
16. Vijayapriya. A
17. Suganeswaran. S
18. Nishaliny. R
19. Aruna. B
20. Iniyashree. N
21. Prerana. P
22. Jasmine Banu. A
23. Nandhini. G
24. Aruthra Ravi
25. Jayalakshmi. S
26. Harshitha. N
27. Sudhiksha. K
28. Arya. S. Nair
29. Deepikha. B
30. Priyanka Singh

31. Shaily Shrivastava
32. Abirami Kaviarasan
33. Caroline Felicita. L
34. Akshaya. M
35. Soundarya Janaki. A
36. Sibiraj. M
37. Santhiya. S
38. Meghna Chatterjee
39. Krithika. S
40. Arpan Shrivastava
41. Cibi T R
42. Monisha Ganesan
43. Sumita Nath
44. Shruthi Aravindakshan
45. Jyoti Jangir
46. Gowri Mahalakshmi
47. Dhanushya. P
48. Yamini Sona Vaishnavi
49. Sneka. K
50. Sirisha Susarla
51. Shakthi Karunanidhi
52. Priyadharshini. T
53. Adhithya
54. Tamilarasi Harikumar. R
55. Sr. Sujatha Balaswami. N
56. Diotima Bose
57. Shruti Agarwal
58. Kayal. R
59. Rupa Bharti
60. Kirubavathi Visvaraj. S
61. Lohitha Devi Maddipoti
62. Bhavika Dhiraj Sindhi
63. Uma Rajmohan
64. Neelukiran

Shubham Shah

(Founder- Flairs and Glairs)

Shubham Shah, an entrepreneur at "Flairs & Glairs" a brand with dynamics in events organizing and cultural educational pan INDIA, is a 26yrs old guy who recently has entered the digital platform of imprinting emotions. He has initiated with his own open mic platform to help budding poets and aspiring writers under his brand named as "Teekhe Zasbaaat"

He is a commerce graduate from the Bhagalpur City of Bihar.
He states Writing has impersonated him since childhood and he has now been writing for over a decade!
Cooking, on the other hand, is his passion! He also mentions, trying out new things just tickles him!
When asked sir, Why SPICY EMOTIONS?
He smiled and added, “agar jasbaat teekhe na ho toh wo jasbaat kahan” Spices are all that blends! So do his words!
As a chef, he presents to you his dish! Hot and freshly served! Taste it! Feel it! Enjoy it! You can also find his writing in the Book “Teekhe Zasbaaat” and 50+ Co-authored anthologies. With his passion to explore opportunities across Platforms, he is working with keen devotion and We wish him all the very best for his future ventures.
He is Featured in the International Magazine DeMode for his upcoming solo novel.
He is Approved by Ne8x for its Lit Fest, and is a Golden Star Awards 2020 Winner.
He is a India Book of Records Holder for his Anthology Satrang, and has the Grandmaster title by Asia Book of Records, for the same.
He has also been featured in Prabhat Khabar, Dainik Jagran, and a lot of other Newspapers in Bihar for his achievements.
He has been a proud co-author to
India Book Of Records (Title- Black)
World Book Of Records (Title -15 Wonders of Poetries)
India Book Of Records (Title - Aaina)
Vajra World Records Holder (Title - Gustakhi Maaf Hai)
High Range of Records Holder (Title - Gustakhi Maaf Hai)
Indian Book of Records
(Title - Road from Worst to Best)

Share your reviews on his

INSTAGRAM

@spicy_emotions
@shubham4shah

Or via email on

shubham2shah@gmail.com

To stay tuned to his work and opportunities follow his business Handles

INSTAGRAM FACEBOOK YOUTUBE

@flairsandglairs
@teekhezasbaaat

WEBSITE:

https://flairsandglairs.in/
https://flairsandglairs.com/

Ishani Agarwal

(Co-Founder- Flairs and Glairs)

Ishani Agarwal hails from the City of Joy, Kolkata.
She is the co-founder of her Community "Teekhe Zasbaaat" and Flairs and Glairs Publication.
Been a Compiler for 45+ Anthologies, she is in the process for more. Co-authored in 150+ Anthologies. She is a India Book of Records Holder, a Vajra World Records Holder, a High Range of Records Holder, an OMG Book of Records Holder, a Bravo Record holder, a Forever Star Book of World Records and an Indian Book of Records Holder.
Approved by Ne8x for its Lit Fest 2020, and Literary Icon 2020. Also a Golden Star Awards Winner 2020.
She has also been awarded with India Star Republic Award 2021, a part of She Awards by Awards Arc and Winner of Nari Samman 2021 by Literoma.

She is also selected as Best Achiever of the Year by AwardsArc and Most Challenging Compiler Award by Spectrum Awards.
She got her first solo Published,a solo Compilation consisting of first 750 contents of hers, titled "Hand That Burnt While Healing".

She has been featured by the National Magazine "Taree Zameen Par" with the title 'unstoppable'.
Also featured in the International Magazine DeMode for her upcoming solo novel, she is proud to write on social issues, and is happy with the love she is receiving.
Connect with her on Instagram: @Ishani_agarwal_quotes / @compilations_so_far

MUSKAN SHAH
(PROJECT HEAD)

"I follow dreams to make them reality."

Muskan Shah, a girl from Jharsuguda, Odisha. Currently a Company Secretary Professional Student, and an Interior Designer. She is a writer and poetess. Being a writer, she writes all genres like stories, articles, quotes, contents, etc. And being a poetess, she writes poetries and they are her forte. Her journey date has been amazing by being a compiler of 10 anthologies and a co-author of 50+ anthologies.
(Instagram @theunpublishedink)

SUBANANTHINI. R
(COMPILER)

"Beauty reveals when you are pure"

Subananthini is currently pursuing her undergraduate degree in Department of English, PSG College of Arts and Science. She is a co-author of 10+ anthologies and co-compiler of 2 anthologies. She is passionate about penning her thoughts without regrets and she hopes to continue her writing forever. She posts her write-ups in Instagram @mist_of_words.

(Instagram @subarajarethinam)

THE FANTASIZER

Every morning, his smile is brighter than the sun,
And I do wish, I could be his only one
I envy the people around him,
Whenever he talks, I used to overwhelm
I have been crazy about his actions,
And I fall for his every reaction
He is not as silly as he seems to be,
And I follow him like a buzzing bee
I don't mean to stalk him every day,
But I wish to stick with his righteous way
His gentle strokes can ease my pain,
And I want to try even if I'm the last in line
I adore him more than anyone,
But, I don't want him to know what I have done
The world is wide and I want to be his only bride,
But I realized my fantasy and sighed
I know it's a dream that I never wish to awake,
But I always hope the dream to be real and not fake
Because I admire him not only in my dreams,
But unconsciously in reality also, it seems.

CHRISTY GNANA DEEPA
(CO-COMPILER)

Christy Gnana Deepa, 20, is hailing from Tamilnadu, India and now residing in Madurai for her studies. She is indeed delightful to thank God at this very moment. Her journey till date is amazing by being a compiler of 5 anthologies and a co-author of more than 40+ anthologies. She is a writer by passion and a literarian by profession. She posts her write-ups on Yourquote, Instagram and NBlik. You can follow her on Instagram for more write-ups.

(Instagram @___budding___writer)

I ADMIRE

"Admire", the great optimistic word,
That can overcome every sword;
The person with a bold heart
And forever over smart;

She cares for me on an extreme level,
She even safeguards me from every trouble,
Once such irretrievable person is my mother'
She is my glory forever!

Besides, I admire the beauty of the Lord,
My strength and my energy
He is my strength when I am weak,
He is my all in my endeavours.

Admire and glorify everyone you see,
Praise and rejoice for their love and care towards you.

MUTHUSELVI. R

She is from Sivakasi, Tamil Nadu. She did her MA., MPhil. Now she is working as an Assistant Professor in SSDM College, Kovilpatti, Thoothukudi District.
(Instagram @baby_nudhal)

THE PERSON YOU ADMIRE

That day, the month of Monsoon
Snowy twilight we passed

Time to see the pleasant warmth of the yellow sun
Your speech is strong enough to amaze

All your first sight, pleasant warmth, naughty talk, mesmerizing smile,
I will never forget the second I saw you

Where did this quick love within us come from?
I live in a world only of full love

That makes me pinch whenever you are with me
No words to say about this relationship with you

The heavier heart goes lighter whenever you hold my hands
Then suddenly the pain comes just to get rid of my hands

But you hide your pain and comfort me with your words
I feel your pain more than your words

Sometimes, our division makes me imprisoned
Do not let my hands turn into wings and join you

That makes my mind long for you
Remove the harsh words and inject clear knowledge into me

You always said to Read On and Move On your life to achieve
I'm trying to let your dream come true

The feeling of heartfelt love has never been seen in anyone
Embracing is going to cross the mind with a lovable touch

Because, the time of withdrawal may at the moment
The Lord was everything to me before I saw you

And I realized he was in me, but I couldn't feel his love for me
Something strange made him to give his love from you to me

Knowing that life is full of surprises and miracles
I find my happiness in every action of you

I want to be your beloved and wish to live with you
I like to carry our memories with me on the melting days and nights

My mind knows the reality, but it can't bear to live apart
Your every actions stay within my soul that never fade away

In my life, I've gone through all the pains and sufferings
But the beauty of our love is to let me live in peace

Because of you, only spring can pass my life
Oh my beloved! I will never forget you

How crazy am I to admire you!
But I wish my craziness to be forever for you

Without you I am incomplete
Because you are damn special to me.

SOMEONE YOU ADMIRE

DEAR!

I feel pleasure to have you in my life and I only admire you the most
I won't say I like you

You are like a beautiful flower and I don't want to pluck it
I admire you for being like a flower

I want to water my love for you
Because I like you more than that I love you

A beautiful flower that stands at a distance and sinks into the plant with its Fragrance!

I enjoy keeping you in your own place without being touched at all Dust in my eyes, I say so

When my eyes felt tears by your memory
Sometimes I miss you!

Just felt how it feels to be without you
Yes! Without you! I feel absurdity!

I feel empty and it's just empty
I love your pampering

I love your scolding

I love your caring

I love your hating

Whatever it is I love you and you only!
Just be with me

I wish to admire you forever
Within Me or Without in front of Me

I want you totally!

Just be with me forever dear.
Hey! Crazy love of me! Please be with me!

Just be with me!

I just need our colourful days
Bring back our memories

Love me or hate me…
I want you to be with me baby!

I need healthy relationship between us till lifelong
The vacuum of the flute is your mind!

Like Music!

Piercing the air that gets lost in the holes
Your love for me makes me feel good,

Refreshing my mind and soul.
I REALLY ADMIRE YOU! MY BABY!

THE BELOVED OF MY SOUL

I have reached a state of real incomprehension
And live in your memory

Your momentary division is also destabilizing
Giving too much time is not enough
You are my first and last of my life

Everywhere I look for you, yet the moment I see you, you disappear
Now the situation separates us
But life is roundabout and we meet again

Some hour you have come and gone
Oh! Lightening, my sky is searching for you
Like a poet searching for his words

I will love you still, though I have to wait
Even though our path changes
And sometimes, I fear of our affection disappearing
Yet, I feel our separation creates our love stronger

For me admiring you is not like praising someone
It is like adoring my love for you
And my admiration for you will never stop
Dear Beloved!

DIVYADHARSHINI. R

An M.A., English and Bachelor of Education graduate. Born on 15th May, 1995 in Honnatty, Kotagiri, Nilgiris. (Instagram @onr_div)

A LADY WHO GONE FAR

Hails from Multan resides Karnal,
Fascinated by planes and flying,
Graduated from Tagore school,
Settled as an Aerospace Engineer.

Began working at NASA Centre,
Applied for an Astronaut corps,
First mission was victory,
While second mission fails.

Died with six humans,
Exists in billion hearts,
Revoking everyday haunts,
Starring blank space of stars.

Buildings named as you,
Your debut pricks and searches,
Nowhere I can find you,
As such other people do.

Everything shattered into pieces,
And so you became ashes,
Million of dreams exhausts,
You rested in peace in heaven.

Your tombstone carried Kalpana Chawla,
As well as hearts of mortals,
Achievement noticed and grasped,
Teary eyes but searches you again.

VASANTHA RANJANI. R

Vasantha Ranjani R is from Trichy, Tamil Nadu. She is a literature graduate with a passion towards language and psychology. She loves to read and write. She is a music lover.

(Instagram @alwayz_ranisa)

ME INSIDE ME

All to myself and you,
Seeing each other everyday
Makes a difference to cherish
For lifetime achievement.
You keep boosting my strengths
Narrow my emotions and feelings
Broaden the path of my walk
Glorify my medals and awards
Never let me down with
Gained popularity and mere fame
Restrained me from the crown
Should I thank you or me?
You live within me,
Inspire me as always,
Weren't you and I same?
With this question lingering,
Thank you my cheerful,
Motivating and encouraging
My dear inner-me.

UMAMAHESWARI. K

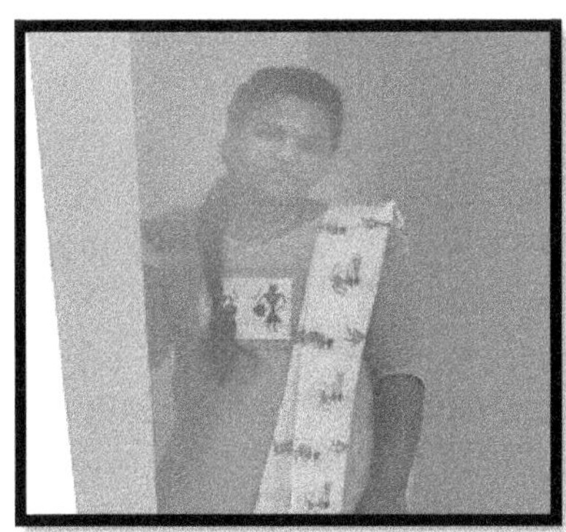

K.umamaheswari is a poem writer who has more creativity and she is passionate with writing stories and she likes to grab more books and wishes to write more fabulous stories and poems.
(Instagram @Tamizh_scrittories)

DEAR "FATHER

He is the one who Adjusts me all the time.
He is the one who Believes me in any situation.
He is the one who Cares me more than others.
He is the one who Developed me in all my bad times.
He is the one who is Enthusiastic to me always.
He is not my Friend.
He is my Father!
You may not carry me for 10 months in your womb.
But, you still carry me in your precious heart
And bear me in your strongest shoulder.
You are my words of wisdom,
Your struggles are my lessons,
Your pains are my experience,
And your kindness is my strength.
You are my inspiration and I Love you the most dad!

CHARULATHA V

Charulatha. V is from Salem, Tamil Nadu. She is pursuing her UG in PSG College of Arts and Science. She is an active reader who loves to read novels and comics. She is the person who loves solitude. She is a budding writer who likes to explore the world in different perspectives.

(Instagram @charulatha677)

ADMIRE YOURSELF

If you take a decision,
There will be a person to confuse you
If you feel happy,
There will be a person to upset you
If you are depressed,
There will be a person to add it more for you
If you are in trouble,
There will be a person to make it double
If you fail,
There will be a person to laugh at you
If you succeed,
There will be a person to take credits for you
Whatever you do,
There will be a person to mislead you
Amidst them, there is a person
Who supports you, guides you and loves you
And that person is YOU
Just do what your heart says,
If you can't, just go with the flow
And the Almighty will lead you to the best.
Encourage your own success,
As your life is something only you can access
No matter what people says
Be who you really are,
Because only you can admire yourself more than any.

MISBAH ISMAIL

Misbah Ismail is from Salem, Tamil Nadu. She is a fashion designing student who views the world in different perspectives. She is passionate to write whatever she feels. (Instagram @ Ismailkarim34)

THE SELFLESS SOULS

My admiration, My Parent
The Architectures, who compromise their comfort and passion as sacrifice;
Incessant to sculpt their masterpiece over precise.
The authors, who compose their edition with dreams,
hopes and joy; bound with everlasting love, desires
And no one can destroy.

The selfless souls, whose love is peace
and need not be acquired; no doubt!
It is humorous, amiable and cannot be measured.
The procreators, who fill their child's bucket of self esteem so high;
That rest of the world cannot poke through holes and drain it dry.

The well springs, whose affection and care is made of deep devotion;
Has no beginning or no end, gives delight and mashed with emotion.
The begetters, whose goodness is higher than the mountain
And their love is deeper than the sea;
Their love is lifelong commitment to selflessness and to be endured with glee.

Their affection is like a deep abyss at bottom,
Of which you always find forgiveness and patient;
Defines the actual definition of beauty, gratitude, power, majesty and proficient.
Their compassion is always whole, no matter how many times divided;
They protect to let us feel secured and their gesture gets multiplied.
The telepathists, who understand us more than our self;
Their affection is the concern for life itself.

SATHISH BALAKUMARAN S.N.I

Mr. S.N.I Sathish Balakumaran completed his UG in Ayya Nadar Janaki Ammal College, Sivakasi (Virudhunagar District), Tamilnadu and he completed his PG in PSG College of arts and science, Coimbatore. Tamilnadu. He completed his M. Phil at Bharathidasan University, Trichy, Tamilnadu. Now he is pursuing his part time Ph.D in VHNSN College, Virudhunagar. He is working as an assistant professor in S.S. Duraisamy Nadar Mariammal College, Kovilpatti (Thoothukudi District), Tamilnadu. He presented and published papers in various Internationals and national conferences.
(Instagram @sni_sbk_official)

SECRET OF MY SUCCESS

I may not belong to them,
Though am from them;
I may not be like them,
Though am totally theirs;
They teach and preach me
Which may sometimes be taken;
They pray and sacrifice their aura
To bring shine to mine;
They punish at times
To make me a man;
Was furious at them
Though they showered love;
Being them is unrealizable
But trying is always the
Power gave by their love.
Pride moment for them
Lies in success of my life.
I succeeded by the
Magical words from them.

LAKXANA. S

Lakxana S is from Erode, TamilNadu. She is pursuing her UG in PSG College of Arts and Sciences, Coimbatore. She is a budding writer who loves to write the world. She likes to be the people's poet. She is not a famous writer but strives to one.

(Instagram @slakxana)

I ADMIRE THE PERFECTLY IMPERFECT.

I admire every X chromosome,
That won a race with Y.
I admire every girl fetus,
Who has just escaped an abortion.

I admire every girl,
Who has broken her love for her family's greed.
I admire every widow,
Who has coloured her white to bright.

I admire every single mom,
Who is raising a child alone, under every nameless pressure.
I admire every pregnant with loosened pelvis,
For the sake of extending her husband's progeny.

I admire every mother,
Who turned her blood to milk to feed her baby.
I admire every divorcee,
Who is determinant to face the world alone.
I admire every homemaker,
Who manages her household, everyday.

I admire every girl,
Who bears menstrual cramps, until her menopause.
I admire every girlfriend,
Who stood against her society for her love.
I admire every spinster,
Who is still enjoying her single life.

I admire every uncovered face of acid attack survivor,
Who exposed her determination as beauty.

I admire every rape survivor,
Who turned her pain into motivation.

I admire every bride,
Who has to replace her in-laws as parents.
I admire every working women,
Who perfectly juggles their job and household.
I admire the entire mother earth,
Who bears all such wonder women.

HEMALATHA. M

M.Hemalatha is a student of Fatima college, Madurai, Tamilnadu. She is currently taking up a bachelor degree in English Literature. She has done her schooling at Jayam Matric Higher secondary school, Villupuram, Tamilnadu. She is a good speaker and participated in many cultural events. She likes reading books and listening to people. (Instagram @Nithya_Kalyani)

MY EXEMPLAR IN LIFE

She was neither born in cot nor in crib
No liabilities held the tiny pretty creature
Her quirking grin detached her parent's melancholy
Neither candles nor balloons blown on her birthday
She commenced her education with full of enthusiasm
The uniform fashioned her like princess
She absorbed compact knowledge about the world
She flied high in intermediate schooling
Her further curiosity in singing moulded her life
People's appreciation stimulated her to shine further
No ailments pulled her downwards
With lot of aches and studiousness she blossomed
She entranced in to new castle for higher studies
A new gang accompanied her
Her accomplishments never ended
Though neglected continuously, a new job knocked her
Family's sufferings made her to toil hard
She carried huge obligation with her
She brought up her family with full hope and desire
Her career as a preacher inspired numerous
Her eloquence and attainment cherished me
She proved achievement didn't expect richness
Her dedication towards passion is priceless
One of those wonder women is you, my sis!

PRIYANKA. R

Priyanka. R is from sivagangai, Tamilnadu. She is pursuing her UG in Karpagam College of Pharmacy, Coimbatore. She is an aspiring pharmacist who loves to pen her thoughts. She is passionate in her writings and won several awards in poetry competitions.
(Instagram @mera_naam_pia)

MY REFLECTION

In this world, there are people, who make wonders,
And she, herself is a wonder who never bothers about her blunders
She is like a sky,
That people likes to see, though it is high
Being confident is her only image,
And it is as good as a tasty vintage
Playing the role of a cool person,
She loves to have her own reasons
She never bothers about her depressions,
Because she is a person with positive expressions
She strives to be someone who never falls,
And she will rise like a sun from her downfalls
Now, she stands in front of me,
Admiring like a humble bee
Seeing her own, she feels blessed,
She always wishes to do her best
And she is my reflection,
Who reflects my own action
And I'm in front of my mirror,
Seeing all my silly errors
And just for that, I wish I could adore her forever.

THARANI. U

She is Tharani, a literature student. She is writing under her pen name Miss Literature.
(Instagram @_pen_downed_thoughts)

THE EMBER IN THE DARK: MY TEACHER

You are an ember in the dark,
The glimpse of you made the spark.
On the day of our first encounter,
Anticipated the changing course of life.

Learnt a little to walk,
Not well-learnt to talk.
With tears of ocean in eyes,
I stepped out of my house.

Even though, the sun shines bright,
World appears as gloomy as night.
Hope not, to meet a soothing soul;
You are the Ember in the dark.

Have met a soul of divinity,
Out from disease of inability.
Sensed the shine of wisdom,
And played the role of prism.

Unaware of divine toxicated soul,
Can change one's life cool.
And brighter than sunshine,
The universe has never dreamt of.

Chanting God can be a prime duty;
For that, words should be taught.
Invocation of muse, done by words;
Saved in memory, learnt from hers'.

Highlighter of good deeds,
Keeps updated as Google.
Both the marble and sculptor
Taught us to be the same.

VIJAYAPRIYA. A

Vijayapriya Amirthamuthu is a student pursuing her undergraduate degree in English literature at PSG College of arts and science at Coimbatore. She is an ardent lover of literature and reality. Her writings are filled with positive approach and hope. The reader should read between lines to get her.
(Instagram @slave_of_pen)

FEATHER OF ADVENTURE

It was the evening of delight
Because I met her for the first time
She,
Looked like the daughter of snow
Walked like the princess of breeze
Smiled like the sister of lily
Spoke like the cousin of rhythm
But actually she is the,
Mother of hope in exerting
Queen of fire in ruminating thoughts
Birthplace of valour in decisive
Devil of potent in endeavour
She is neither bed of roses nor thorns
She is the feather of adventure
Dear reader, Stop reading!
Otherwise she will admire you too

EXPLAINING THAT MOMENT

I dare explaining the moment when
My eyes caught you for the first time
Your appearance was awesome that
I wondered if you dressed so well only to kill me
That attitude you carried was made by
Buoyancy of rose tinted glasses
Someone poured music into my ears
That you were my family friend
Your exclusive "hello" made me
Grin like a Cheshire cat
That hour with you was magical
Like a dog with two tails
But your farewell made me get
Tied up in knots
Dear reader, Stop!
Did you get a person in your soul while reading this?
If so, that person admires you the most

SUGANESWARAN. S

He is a nutritionist. And a time pass writer of his life experience. He is interested to motivate himself and others. (Instagram @love_on_photography_8_official)

LIVING ANGELS

In the shades of darkness of society,
Women glow like a star
In the black side's of family,
Women scatter the colours of life
In the routine life of quarrels,
Women lead the work space
In the universe of brutal evils,
Women walk like an angel
In the pain of breaking bones,
Women nurture the little one
In the world full of inferiority,
Women chauvinism results in success
In the body full of pain and spasms,
Women ignore and simply move on
And I admire them
For their sacrifice,
For their simplicity
And for their perseverance.

FAILURE

From the dark town of failure
The success city has formed
From the sad sides of failure
The strong hearts are formed
From the stairs of failure
The hard minds are formed
From the tears of failure
The Truth are formed
From the taste of failure
The courage is formed
From the pain of failure
The faith is formed
From the life of failure
The lessons are taught
From the shames of failure
The new man is born!!
And I admire that man
Who has won all his failures.

NISHALINY R

She is a person who wants to explore everything.
(Instagram @nishaliny_ramesh1414)

SALT AND PEPPER

No matter what they
Brought to you
No matter how they
Influence you
No matter why they started to spy on you
No matter when they
Made you pen your thoughts
No matter where you
Begin all these things
Everything in life is salt and pepper
Which is not an exact measure
But matters "who" did all the above
Not only loyalty admires you
But also betrayal do

ARUNA. B

B.Aruna is doing her UG in S.S.Duraisamy Nadar Mariammal College, Kovilpatti (Tuticorin District), Tamilnadu. She likes to recite poems and she is interested on writing poems. She likes to read Historic novels. She likes to go for a road trip.
(Instagram @Aruna balaganesh)

MY BOOSTING FIRE FLY

You are the person that I most admire,
The person that I would like to be.
Your friendship is like a torch that lit a fire.
Deep within the cave where I am me.
Because of you,
I want to be a teacher,
Touching someone's life as you have touched mine.
Giving her the faith from which she can shine.
Though you must leave now, and we must part,
A little piece of you remains behind,
Held with gratitude within my heart,
A portrait of a good and kind lady.
When I need strength, I will look for you inside.

INIYASHREE. N

Iniyashree is currently pursuing her undergraduate in PSG College of arts and science, Coimbatore. Her hobby is to write poems.
(Instagram @Ini_naresh_)

MY IDOL

She didn't ask me can I help?
But told me I'll help.
She didn't tell me what to write,
But told me how to write.
She didn't tell me not to talk,
But she told me how to talk.
She told me not to be distracted by look,
But to get all the extract from the book.
She told me not to measure,
But to get a treasure with much pleasure.
Everything she taught me had a moral within
She took me from darkness to light
And gave the knowledge of might
She never asked me to seek admiration
But, I got admired.
She is someone special to me!

PRERANA P

Prerana is a budding poet born in the year 2002. Though resides in Tamil Nadu, she is a native of Kerala. She is deeply interested in Poetry, Music and Public speaking. Being an Aspiring Artist, she loves to learn new skills and art each day.
(Instagram @love_whatu_love)

I CHOOSE ME

How pretty she looks,
How handsome he looks,
Is all we think about,
Throughout the way.

Attires she has,
Stunning goggles he has,
Is all we notice about,
Throughout the way.

Take a break,
Turn to your mirror,
Then we realize,
We missed out the gem.

Of course, we look upon others,
Of course, our mind spins faster,
But it's always fine,
To recess and relish our SELF.

I admire the way I sing,
I dance, I gossip, I shout,
I sneeze, I talk, I laugh,
The list goes to what not.

To face the struggles,
To enjoy the results,
Admire every bit of self,
That's where the heaven settles.

JASMINE BANU. A

A free spirited person with lots of curiosity and aspires to become a writer. And she loves to travel.

SOMEONE I ADMIRE

He was indeed a Keyser Sóze.
For still he kept himself hidden!!
He was a pure thinker
For believing in e-money freedom.
He was a pioneer in cryptography
For he created a winged dime.
He was sheer breathed person
For he vanished in shadows.
He was one of the greatest minds in the world
As he has to create something like that!!!
Still he likes to keep himself underground
Even if he found an unimaginable and awesome idea
which is now true
A legend with potential to convince the world that he didn't
exist at all Still in this world, he is a shadow
Who is Satóshí Nakamoto, in the name which he calls
himself!

NANDHINI. G

She completed her Bachelor of Arts in English literature. She is a blogger.

DUALITY ADMIRATION

Is she Athena or Aphrodite
Or Venus in disguise.
Is she the mermaid of brooks
Or the enchanter of looks.
Does she smell lavender or roses
Is her smile more enriching than proses.
Is she a woman with braided hair and gentle exposure
Or does she battle with shining armour with enrapture.
Is she a woman of innate wisdom
Or does she acts according to the custom.
Can her words stir reformation among us
Or does it bring revolt and fuss.
Does her expression surpass the sunshine
Or her devotion make her outshine.
Charismatic and enigmatic, a parallel universe she displays.
I admire the duality, a blend of night and day.

ARUTHRA RAVI

This is Aruthra Ravi. Her journey as a writer began when she discovered her inner talent as "playing with words " to convey her feelings , opinions and also sort down undeniable facts .Her writings are in the form of Quotes, facts and poems. She firmly believes that if we start following our passion, we will shine bright one day though it takes time to strengthen our talents that's how we discover a stronger new version of ourselves.
(Instagram @for_my_soulmates)

THE PERSON I ADMIRE IS, "GOD AS A SCULPTOR OF HUMAN".

God trusted man even before he gave life:
Human doubted God even after he got life as man.
Omnipotent God believed human undoubtedly:
Intelligent Human doubted God frequently!
God gave man sense to do business:
Man gave God cents from his business!
God began blessing human that's the beauty of eternity!
Man began cursing God that's the heights of Stupidity!
God blesses the needy : teaches the greedy:
Man believes the greedy: deceives the needy
Man trades with God's temple:
God grades the Human's temple (Brain)
Crazy humans attract God!
Lazy humans distract God.
God can do anything without help of human,
Man can do nothing without help of God!

God plays with human to teach!
Human plays with money to preach!
While God acts and man reacts, these are tests!
While Man acts and God reacts, these are lessons!
Speaking out our worries to God, we get relaxed!
Speaking out God's worries to us, we would get startled!
That's why God teaches human
Human preaches God's words
Man bribes to get blessings:
Imagine if God bribes to give blessings!
Humans are blessed with the power of attraction!
God tests our power with small distraction!
It's high time to thank God,
Who blessed us to be born as "Human"
So we can thank him every second of life!

JAYALAKSHMI. S

She is doing her final year (UG) in literature. She is interested in writing.
(Instagram @jay_chamamanda)

THE ARTIST'S ART

We are all an art
By the artist, the God
We will become an artist
When we admire the art of God.
Admiring is an art
That makes everyone smart.
Eyes are made to admire
I use it wisely, ready to swear.
The top most gangster
Venerated for his master mind,
That makes the problem to wind.
I also esteem the artist
For their taste of choosing
The artist's art.
Somehow If you are linked with me,
Then be proud that you are admired by me.

HARSHITHA. N

This is Harshitha, final year undergraduate student in English literature. She believes that she can give life to her past through her words and inks her thoughts to show people what they missed in this fast-moving world.
(Instagram @__harshitha_05)

THAT ONE PERSON

We all have that one person
Who comes to our mind
When something happened in our life!

Life changed lively and colourful
when I met that person

I am not sure how it started but,
One thing for sure, it's never going to end!

In the world of fake people,
She became my human dairy

I admire her
not for her smile,
though it makes me positive
not for her care,
though it never made me to feel alone
But for her selflessness,
The way she is - more than that
it's our fellowship- I admire a lot!

She lit a fire in my life
that doesn't burn me,
It burnt what I am not
revealed what I am!

When I want to give up everything,
She made me to start everything
When I went in a wrong direction,
She hand me a new direction
We shared a lot almost everything,

but not those samosas
And that's our bond!

We are not bonded by red binding
We are bonded by brown roots!

SUDHIKSHA. K

Sudhiksha is a fervent reader, who has an appetite for Contemporary Young Adult Fiction and Fantasy novels. She started her reading mania with the Harry Potter series at the age of 9 and her love for reading has grown ever since. She is a credible orator and an excellent debater. She likes role-playing and has played the characters of Mark Antony and Jo March in dramas. She has also published short-stories across Wattpad. Apart from reading, her favourite pastime is coding programs and designing web pages. Some of the all-time treasures that lines her bookshelves are: The Stormlight Archives, The Infernal Devices, and Throne of Glass. Her poem is about the protagonist of the Throne of Glass series, Aelin Galathynius, whom she considers to be her inspiration.
(Instagram @the_dauntless_archeron_17)

FIREHEART

Born from ashes and forged in fire;
Raised by brigands to become an assassin;
She was the lost princess, Brannon's heir;
She loved her kingdom with all her heart.

Her spirit could never be broken;
She did not fear, she did not falter.
The seraphim in her had awoken;
She was Fireheart and she did not yield.

She lit up the darkest of all paths;
The Queen of flame and shadows.
Light and embers in her eyes she hath;
A heart full of Wildfire she possessed.

She was a dreamer, a fighter;
She bowed for no one and nothing.
She was destined to burn brighter;
She challenged the sky and the stars.

She inspirited me to rattle the stars;
And propelled me to be a dreamer among empirics.
She taught me to embrace my flaws and scars;
And reminded me not to let the hard days win.

Like a phoenix she has arisen,
From dust and smoke and shadow;
All hail the Queen of Terrasen,
Aelin Ashryver Galathynius !

ARYA. S. NAIR

Arya, is currently doing her MA in English Literature. She is also pursuing her MSc. Yoga along with it. An ardent reader, she is highly influenced by the Indian Poet Kamala Das. She is also a passionate writer. Her articles are published in her blog page titled GirlTalk. Also interested in analyzing various works, she has presented papers in two colleges, namely, SIES College of Arts and Science, Sion, Mumbai and Nirmala College for Women, Coimbatore. Her writings mostly concentrate on various social issues and human emotions. A keen advocate of equality, she strongly believes that the world will become a place worth living only when people are respected and treated well regardless of their gender, caste or colour.
(Instagram @arya_9802)

EACH ONE

That man I saw helping his old mother try on her favorite dress,
The lady who paid her currently unemployed boyfriend's bill,
The man who chose to look after his house,
The woman who sat beside her crying friend who broke his heart,
The parents who whole heartedly allowed their son to wear a saree,
The brother who allowed his sister to marry a girl,
The family that let their daughter marry out of caste,
The child who did not laugh at his friend with white patches,

Each one of them is someone I admire,
Each one a humane human.

DEEPIKHA. B

Deepikha has completed her M.A English Literature. She is interested in reading books and watching movies. She is residing in Coimbatore.
(Instagram @Deepikha barathan)

MY INSPIRED MODEL

Sports a special part of some,
The bat created a Batsman,
The Ball created a bowler,
The Ground created Players,
The Game known to be Cricket,
A team of Eleven:
Ready to play in ground,
Many cricketers attracted Many,
But,Viratkohli took me away,
A passionate, hard worker.
The handsome, young Ardent player,
As Batsman in Junior Indian team,
Then, reached IPL,
As captain of Royal Challengers Bangalore,
A batsman of International Indian team,
Now, the Captain of ICC India,
Who caught the eyes of many,
Is my Epitome of Dedication,
Passion and strong effort was learned,
Which made me study hard and endure,
And one day I'm sure,
I will reach great heights on my Goal.

PRIYANKA SINGH

Priyanka is an HR Professional holding educational degrees from Christ University and Amity University. She has worked for Microsoft in the past and was an entrepreneur for a small business. Now she is settled in Berlin and exploring her passion for writing.
(Instagram @Baby.blabber)

TANTALIZING AROMA OF MY MOM'S PERFUME

Like a morning prayer her soul is so pure
Her hug has the magic that gives out cure
Her smile is lovely like a beautiful rosebud
In her laughter, fades away the worldly hubbub

As a kid, I wore from her bottle of perfume and
Tippity-Tapped around the house in her high heeled shoes
Draped her stole like a "lehenga choli"
I pretended to be her, in front of my siblings
And though I own a fine collection now
I just love to sneak in her dresser to find out how her favourite perfume smells like
And did I grow into her shoes that I like

A TWITE IN MY LIFE

Early in the morning, when the sun is not so bright
I hear a sound, falling on my ears very light
It's such a delight, when you wake me like a twite
Calling me mama like a melodic recite

Giggling and wiggling like a jingling bell
Your laughter sounding like a singing nightingale
Casting a magic spell in our story tale
The tintinnabulation of your mellifluous voice
The innocuous argument with your toys
The annoyance on your face
The infectious laughter you wear
Holding my finger you twirl like Miss Claire
You are my darling daughter for who I will always be there

SHAILY SHRIVASTAVA

She is an IT consultant loves writing poetries, nature, art and animal lover, maybe one day my photo would be on my book cover.
(Instagram @soulfulpoetry7)

THE ADMIRER

I admire you for what you are
Yeah we were close once now I admire you from afar.
Your face your laugh your sparkling eyes
Did not know your words were all lies
I still admire you for what you are.
If only you could know how those days spent
come crawling back like a dark rainy night,
My heart pound, eyes well up to not agree what seems to be right,
You chose to be free for they say I was a prison,
You told me it was me, who gave you the reason,
Let's settle on one thing; I know you do too,
Yeah I still admire you for what you are!

ABIRAMI KAVIARASAN

Abirami is curious person, who thinks "Life is always full of surprises and lessons and it may show that at any moment, so buckle up and always be ready to experience it ". She enjoys her life in all the possible ways. Abirami is a literature student and a budding writer and poet. "Just smile and let your smile make a difference".
(Instagram @abiramii_ak)

YOU ARE SPECIAL

Not everybody can be
how you are.
Not everybody can do
what you do.
Not everybody is like
who you are.

The way you do things,
The way you treat people,
The way you care for others,
Is something different.
It makes me wonder.

You make me wonder
How to be like you?
How to do things like you?

Later, I realised,
It is something that only you can do.
Just don't care what others tell,
what others do
Coz, they can never be like you.

You are someone special,
Not only for me, but for all.
So, be happy always MY MOM!!!

CAROLINE FELICITA. L

Her name is Caroline Felicita. She's currently studying Post Graduate in English Literature at Fatima College, Madurai. Her native place is Batlagundu. She loves reading and writing. Reading comforts her in all the troubles. And writing creates a happy person in her. Through writing she expresses her thoughts that she cannot express through her lips. She loves to write stories and poems and to read mysterious horror genre books.
(Instagram @Caroline_rosie)

MY NAILED HERO

Yes, He nailed His job given to Him
By saving the world from sin,
Yes, He nailed His job given to Him
By nailing Himself in the cross.
No one knows He failed himself
So I can get that success myself.

He was accused for the mistakes He has never done,
I admired how He didn't defend Himself.
In the path of success, people will accuse you,
But don't try to prove yourself to others.

He was whipped for forty times,
I admired the way He controlled Himself in pain.
In the path of success, there will be whipping and lashing,
But try to accept the pain.

He carried the 136 kg Cross in agony,
I admired the way He carried it without complaining.
In the path of success, there will be a load of responsibilities,
But don't complain about your struggles.

He was nailed in arms and legs,
I admired His passion to save me.
In the path of success, failures will nail you somewhere,
But be passionate about your goal.

He was hanged in the cross without clothes,
I admired that He didn't try to cry in shame.
In the path of success, there will be lot of shame,
But try to accept the humiliation.

His heart was sliced by the spear,
I admired how He remained calm in the pool of blood.
In the path of success, people will stab you in the heart,
But accept the pain of stabbing.

He was died in the cross but resurrected,
I admired the way He didn't fear for death.
In the path of success, do not fear for failure,
So that you can be resurrected into success.

He's the one who inspired me.
He made me what I am now.
He's the person I admire.
He's Jesus Christ.

AKSHAYA. M

Akshaya, Literature student of pondicherry University. She is a quite admiring personality who always finds pleasure in picturing her thoughts. She is a reader by choice and writer by luck. she will work on her happiness and love to see herself in a special setting, doing different things. Though her level is not yet standardized her hungry heart made her to strive with her letters and words. She also draws her attention to music and thinks that music is the only thing that can turns her on.
(Instagram @___akshaya.__)

I ADMIRE HIM:

On his toes, with legs crossed
And cigarettes on-
Buttressed by a street pole,
Posing a sarcastic smile,
Stood a Roadside Romeo.

Holding a "Morning Chronicles"
Arms bursting out from
Roughly half folded shirt,
In hold of enough nerves-
With the fixating fishy eyes,
Reading the headlines- gained
A great sigh of relief.
Brushing the hair backwards,
His enthusiasm never headed down.
Negating any jot of regrets
He moved here, there and
Almost everywhere.

The saddest is - I was clammed up- after
He wildly plunged into me
On that bloody day.
Guilt wrap around me
Like a cold, wet blanket.
I lost what I shouldn't.
Dying between virtue and contempt.
Even then - he continues to
Retain on top of the world.

About to impregnate by a
Don't-know-who-he-is person.
They forbade me constantly

From falling on my desires.
But he- blissfully
Spread his coloured wings.

Living my life to the
Fullest is the sin
As I lack the one he posses.

With all, I admire him- For he
Further on the roads,
Bagging umpteen crimes.
I admire him - For he
Out of that bloody day and
Pointless social criticism.
I admire him - For he
Never reaped what he sown.
I admire him - For he
Remain as an undying embers.
I still admire him.

SOUNDARYA JANAKI. A

She is a Literature student. She is a beginner and an aspiring writer from Madurai, Tamilnadu.
(Instagram @itz_.asj)

SOMEONE AHEAD IN THE TIME!

No particular reason I could think of,
But she's got a vibe like me.
Wilder yet an empath,
Independent, rebellious yet soft-hearted,
Outspoken yet a good listener.
I guess she's not tired of humans.
She may not be as pure as snow but
She's the jar of honey from the hive.
She has learnt to lend smiles.
Create rainbows amongst the greyest clouds.
Desires defined, moving towards her goals,
She has got everything I aspire and adore
I aspire to be her.
I admire her.
I'll become her.
To inspire my past self, like she does now!

SIBIRAJ. M

He is Sibiraj, doing his 3rd B.A.English.
(Instagram @Sibiraj192)

THE RISE OF DICTATOR

The world saw variety of cultures and people,
No one was interested to know but dominance knew,
The history speaks milestones not stones,
Remember what we do, not do for,
Just ask your heart, who take rules to rule,
Questions do not rise but rise in suffer,
Let's see the pain and life of war hero.

A nation in a great stand; outbreak of war,
Dark clouds surrounded at all,
No chance to escape enemies for,
Signed the treaty of Versailles,
Economic conditions brings sufferings,
For only Aryans not foreigns,
Own army kills, own people.

A psychotic man who survive,
Great human war with eagle eyes,
Crying for lose in the war,
As a spy, watch the movement of,
German workers party and blames,
Summit the report to command,
That says, the elimination of Jews.

At first propaganda, brings the attentions,
Step by step, the crowd gathered around,
The fiery speaker, Adolf Hitler makes possible,
To peels the skin of communist government,
People understand what's going on,
Foreign invaders took all from them,
And take over all lives.
The great vision and faith in reality,

Took him to next step to show power,
The fiery speech attract the lost people,
Results are favourable to invaders,
Not to the natives, rise of fires,
Make the change, that change,
Brings the powers from them.

Burning the books to spread,
Communism comes to bury,
The pride spread over all,
Germans feels Germans,
The great stand crush the invasions,
No one can survive from all,
Remaining awaiting list.

Night of broken glass,
Burning light in head office,
The last one comes to second,
No one can believe this,
Chancellor comes out show power,
Death of Hindenburg, feel all,
The birth of Dictator is the third Reich.

The great vision of propaganda,
Rise to power in the Reich,
To see the rise of evil risen,
Seig Heil! Seig Heil! Seig Heil!

SANTHIYA. S

Santhiya is from Thoothukudi, Tamilnadu. She has completed her B.A., B.Ed. She is a budding poet who has an interest on writing poem as her passion.
(Instagram @_choco.pop_)

MY BOLD LADY

To my precious angel,
You are the precious gift in my life,
I'm writing you this poem,
Mom, you are the best example of love, care and support,
My bold lady, I would send my love through this poem,

You are my strong pillar,
Your motivation and encourage make me to do everything,
My dreams are like little seed,
You encourage and nurture to grow me like a beautiful tree,
Your love is like my blood cells which always make me active,

Oh, my lovely queen, you treat me as a princess,
You are the first person to hold my hands,
Every day you protect me as a little chicken,
Now, I've grown up, but still you handle me as a child,
You are my first teacher, friend even you are my first adviser,

As my first teacher,
You let me to grow my own wings,
You take my dream as yours,
Backbone of me face more struggle in my pathway,
For your contribution is immeasurable.

As my first friend,
The only person stands in my happy and sad days,
For many times, you hide your pain
And walk with my horrible situation,
Every day I scold and sought you
But your care and love is not less than me.

I know you are my precious angel,
Our relationship is apart from the world,
Like my DNA, our bond has never broken,
I won’t leave you in any situation
Because you are mine, you are my inspiration
And every day I admire you!

MEGHNA CHATTERJEE

She is a simple girl with the simplest dream of spreading smiles and cheers all around. She is pursuing Sociology Honours from St.Xaviers College Kolkata. Being a passionate writer she has worked in more than 15+ anthologies namely, Illusionary Yours, Flashed Rhythm, The Fearless and flawed, My Success Ladder, Unseen Blessings and so on.
(Instagram @Meghna.Chatterjee)

SHE IS AN INSPIRATION

In front of her beauty,
the vibrancy of the luminescent sun fades,
Her aura of an indomitable fervour
unfurls it's petals in exuberant pastel shades.
She isn't any fairy with the most tantalising
lips of crimsons and skin buttery white,
But she is a worrier with a wow indomitable
and the ravaging scars of a fierce fight.
Those while grimaces of an acid attack, rapacious and violent
The contagious beam on her face
withers away the thorns glowing sweet and resplendent.
Her strength as her armour,
Her might as her cape.
In the glistening attire of confidence,
Her jubilant soul would drape.
Plucking away the rapacious thorns of past she thrives,
swirling the cape of optimism and determination.
Busking in the glory of a triumphant rejuvenation.
Unravelling the leaves of smile and compassion
amidst the dried imprints of trauma she slays.
Again and again in front of her chivalrous marvel,
any other beauty of the world mellows down and fades.

KRITHIKA. S

She is Krithika. She is studying BSC Microbiology. She is a nice person to spend time with. She is a good and kind hearted person. She has great talents. She is a very good writer and she is proud of that. She is sincere in all her works. The best thing about her is she never gets depressed or pissed off because of the negative vibes that stop her. She is a person who solely depends on hard work and not has a false hope on luck. On the other hand she works smart too. The best thing about her is that she never gets attracted to the negative vibes surrounding her.
(Instagram @reminisce_with_krtz)

GUIDING LIGHT

Admiring your every move
Above the sky, you are my sunshine
In your presence, everything feels light
Between you, where my joy lies
Tremendously feel awaited
Seeking you in my every decision
Taking your advice is my pleasure
A day without you feels abandoned
Expressing both our views
Lifting our views towards the vision is
Unique and evident to my identity
You share your life with me
Evolve me into the fantasy of castle.

GOLDEN GIRL

Visiting you given me immense pleasure
Following your path makes me successful
Claps have to be given to you
For crafting and craving me in every possible way
Even the thought of meeting you makes them feel happy
You developed me into another person
Taking close to my destiny,
Little steps of my foot move towards you forever
You made my life fantastic
And persisting towards the perfection.

ARPAN SHRIVASTAVA

Arpan is a student of class 12 . With having both huge dreams as well as care for the very small things in his heart. Being a commerce student he has a different perspective towards life, for example considering his family and friends as his biggest assets and negative attitude as the biggest liability.
(Instagram @_._.aceofspades._._)

A FRIEND WHOM I ADMIRE

It's the best friend of mine, whom I admire the most.
In every dark phase, she has been the only constant ray of hope.
Been there in my best as well as in worst times.
Always been the only solution which I could find right.

Met so many people in life, but never found someone as unique as her.
When everyone got frustrated, the patience she had was rare.
Showed me the value of friendship, and how valuable could one person be!
When I got scared of being all alone, she assured me that she is always by my side.

It is her self-confidence, which I admire the most.
No matter how hard the situation get, she never loses hope.
With the constant support, she inspired me to be better every day.
It's the best friend of mine, whom I admire the most.

With all my heart, I am grateful for having a friend who motivates me to be better everyday day.
I hope, somehow I would be able to explain how much this friendship means to me one day.

CIBI T R

He is strongly determined towards the work he has committed. He believes in consistency. He is a nature worshiper and a literature lover.
(instagram @t_r_cb)

MAHATHMA

Pale flower looks dark in the dusk,
Which have blossomed to tease the freedom fragrance!
Morning star of Indian Independence,
Achieved by emitting the light of non-violence.
Thought and aim of Guru is 'Ahimsa'
Ultimate goal to stand with patience,
Struggles underwent is numerous
Result of which is Indian Independence.
His roar echoed the first cabinet,
Thus result is of two women ministers
To empower the women rights
And to upgrade and equip their selves.
That's why he is mahatma!
Whom is the reason for independence aroma!

MONISHA GANESAN

She is a Math tutor. She stepped as torch bearer for future generation. She wishes to view herself in the world of poem.
(Instagram @seeker_ofthoughts)

MY VALOROUS FEMALE WARRIOR

As spooky as Roller coaster,
Your arduous legs climbing a steep slopes,
And diving through sharp curves.
Oh my gallant warrior! Oh my gallant warrior!

As freaky as barn owl,
Your staring eyes in scary night,
To shield our country from nemesis.
Oh my gallant warrior! Oh my gallant warrior!

As plucky as lion,
As optimistic as pilot,
As straight as an arrow,
She stood valiant at frontier.
I admire you, my valorous warrior!

SUMITA NATH

Sumita Nath hails from the City of Joy, Kolkata. She is an Indian author born to a Bengali family. She qualified her graduation in Pharmaceutical Science and MBA in Total Quality Management. Her early life for 20 years spent at Heart of India which is Madhya Pradesh and then moved to different cities of India. In year 2016 she decided to pursue her childhood passion for writing. She started writing rhymic poetries and has a page named rhymic fun. She is a co-author of many anthologies. She is also a You Tuber of KAVITA SVAR SUMITA. She is a working professional in the field of Quality Assurance. She loves cooking and believes in good food brings good mood.
(Instagram @RphSumitaNath)

FAITH TO KISS THE VICTORY CUP

I admire you
In all the view
I look for the motivation
From you without any hesitation
When you to me say
Shape the vase out of the clay
Life is more of twist and turns
Throughout the times you will learn
Many a times you will feel to give up
But it's worth to enjoy the victory cup
There would be times you have doubts
But your believe have strength ins and outs
Many a glorious morning yet to be seen
Have faith to kiss the meadows green.

TO CHASE YOUR DREAM IN LIFE'S RICH STREAM

Here a part of my story which I admire in Plainsong
I am a Bengali bong with Headstrong
And mistakes are made by me too in many Forms
But my family and friends never forget to
Cheer my energy with their Folksong

So I always say
When your past had gone bitter & Wrong,
Family and friends will make it better & Strong
March on - grow on with life's new Song
Turn on the rich stream of joy and float Along

You are blessed to be a Bong
Life had explained you this in many Form
As our culture is so Strong
Our family will never leave us alone for Long

Get up and arrange your life like golden Corn
Don't miss the chance to dance like King Kong
Mark my words for Lifelong
Get up and Chase your dream that Belongs!!!

SHRUTHI ARAVINDAKSHAN

When we fall there should be a good hand to hold us back, not only to motivate and inspire us but also to guide us in the right way. Shruthi Aravindakshan is such a person who would accompany us with her thought provoking words. She started her career as a Montessori school teacher, helping those little hands to spread their wings of hope in the near future. She belongs to orthodox Hindu family where people do not mix up tradition and modernity. She is a good singer and very much fond of music. People love her for the way she is and vise versa. She loves gardening and maintains a small area for that in all the places she lives. She is simple, fun loving and straight forward friend.

FRAGRANCE

It was a busman's holiday,
When I stepped out of my door;
A disturbed feel came into my mind,
That tickled my nose and thought.
I made a welcome wave,

But it vanished in the empty air.
My questing eyes started to spy all-around,
In order to spot-on this unresolved mysticism!
Something that wished to fill
My lonely hours of my bustle day.

My intellectual mind started to
Quibble over some unethical questions,
That was vaguely answered;
Stimulating the un quenching thirst
Of my reasoning heart.

Like a mad huntsman,
I searched, and searched, and searched;
The quest of my eternal search was resolved
By the fresh, sweet smile of a perfect RED ROSE;
Which was laid on the wild path of ETERNITY!

JYOTI JANGIR

Jyoti Jangir is a 23 year old visionary girl with curiosity of knowing different aspects of this beautiful world. She is daughter of open minded parents Rajendra Jangid a carpenter and sharda devi a beautiful housewife who stood strong to make her believe that she deserves eternity of approbation. After completing the post-graduation (M.com), she got a feeling to change the world and make the world much better place to live for those who struggle. During the journey of standing tough, writing became her weapon to be more attentive towards the goal. As a Theist & zoophilist she believes "integrity is an only desideratum for every living being on earth" She wants to become an inspiration to her brother lakshay & other children around the world. She has a faith to prove herself.
(Instagram @sharda_jyoti_soul_of_pureness)

I ADORE YOU MOTHER!

Your love is like a holy river that deepens to very end of the sea.
When there is no end at all!
My soul chirping around you with so much of fascination
Fascination of that peace you make me feel
Wondered by your fighting spirit against every catastrophe
aiming me..! I adore you infinitely!
You catch beautiful hopes and manage to smile with every
sunrise.
I adore you to infinity & beyond!

Your voice each day pacifies my worries every single time
when I get back home just in one shot
Like there was none of it ever felt!
Making real sense, so definite! I adore you mother!
The tranquil and the heartfelt calm of every cuddle
Smoothly running through blood veins of mine
Assuring "nothing can be that bad"
And Justification to all raised query in just that one quote
"I have you on my side!" I adore you mother!

Your presence at the door
Awaiting for me & your welcoming
"Oh my child has come home" is the only reason
For my hurry & rush, so hard to comeback every evening from
work!
I adore you mother!
You've shown rainbows in every season
Once and always, "The most beautiful thing I have ever seen"
Your wonderful motherhood beating every evil eye on me was
purely celestial indeed! I adore you mother!

Scare isn't scary at all when it is affronted with you before
On a way to me!
You staring harsh at God compelling him to look after me every
time

I believe! God has admired you too
I adore you mother!
You making excuses for making me eat more is
Pure and strictly unalloyed!

I love the moment your hand is cushion I fall every night on!
You calming down when things are already set ablaze by me
You are guiding & cleaning all the fogs & everything invisible to me!
You are the only life form without any label
You are so kind to me at that uttermost level! I adore you mother!
You perform perfect & 'no mean'
You are the consummate professional queen!
I bring many clouds of doubts where I casually suffer "How! How!" You always manage to differ! I adore you mother!

You are the moon in the darkest night with hope of something fine
You are so much of that strong lion! I adore you mother!
With the unstoppable confidence she never agrees to hide
Look how wonderful she is every day
She has belongings of heights
Time expanding every moment within her
She is explorer & survivor of realm & so clear!

Light as a beautiful feather
Thoughtful as so many elders have gathered!
She is wonder to many, very bright
Being part of you always makes me feel so much of delight!
I adore you mother!
Looking at the world from your eyes is afar opposite of real night!
I adore you to infinity & bliss
It continues, continues & will never end !

GOWRI MAHALAKSHMI

She is Gowri Mahalakshmi. She is a student pursuing engineering. She is passionate about writing, reading. She owns a page in Instagram (@question.on), she writes blogs (askyourselfpage.blogspot.com), and is also a video creator. She hopes everyone to like and enjoy her write-up by reading them.
(Instagram @screw.perfect.22)

KNOWING BETTER

I never knew he will be my soul-mate,
I just know he will be my mate.
I never knew he can give me butterflies,
I just know he can see through my eyes.
I never knew he can understand my feeling,
I just know he can find this meaning.
I never knew he can kiss my pain,
I just know everything may go in vain.
I never knew he can calm me down,
I just know he won't pull down my crown.
I never knew he can be my everything,
I never knew he can be my king,
I never knew he can be still holding,
I never knew he can be falling each and every time only for me!
I never knew him, yet I admire him!

DHANUSHYA. P

She is a final year English graduate at PSG College of Arts and Science, Coimbatore. She is a budding writer, budding photographer and she is a co-author of more than two anthologies.
(Instagram @words_from_heart_9623, @dhanushya_palaniappan)

NATURE AS AN ADMIRER

I got admired from nature and everything.
It admires from dawn to dusk
Which made me perfect.
It admires from sun to moon
Which made me to shine.

It admires from Earth to sky
Which made me to remain silent.
It admires from plants to trees
Which made me to grow.
It admires from animals to human
Which made me to fight for the right.

It admires from animals to birds
Which made me to fly high in the sky.
It admires from God to Parents
Which made me to live with strength and confidence.
It admires from stories to reality
Which made me to create an epic.

It admires from failure to success
Which made me to work hard.
It admires from school to college
Which made me to be a writer.
It admires from expectations to experience
Which made me to learn a lesson.

It admires from past to present
Which made me to think and act accordingly.
It admires from negativity to positivity
Which made me to think good and great.
It admires from old to modern

Which made me to think creatively new.
It admires from last to first
Which made me to move step by step.
It admires from birth to death
Which made me to understand the value of time.

YAMINI SONA VAISHNAVI

Yamini Sona Vaishnavi is a budding writer who pursues her III UG of English Literature in Madurai, Tamil Nadu. She has a great love for books and writing, especially, poetry and quotes. She started her writing passion right from her school age for yearly magazines and continued the same in her college. Currently she is a co-author for almost 15 anthologies.

YOU DECK OUT YOURSELF FOR ME

Words can never describe the way god created your appearance
He might even fail if he tries to create yet another person like you
You are such an original personality that you can never be substituted
Your sense of dressing just cuts a dash!
And the way you look at things can even put an end to clash!
Though you have that five' O clock shadow on your masculine face,
I never understand, how is that not a hair out of place is possible in your look!
Your hair that looks like a million dollars,
You're pretty as a picture smile,
Your height which is very contrasting to the vertically challenged me,
Looks so adorable and alluring
Even when analysed, it's difficult for the rest to identify your secret! The secret of you being so handsome my Mr. Handsome,
Which only I knew!
It's purely your heart my love which only I understand!
It's a peaceful place where only I live!

SNEHA. K

Sneha.K is a pre final year student pursuing at Sri Ramakrishna College of arts and science for women, Coimbatore and currently taking up a bachelor degree in English language and literature. As a literature student she experiences her life through literature. She completed her schooling at Infant Jesus Matric. Hr. Sec. School, Coimbatore. She belonged to top 5 ranks of high school and higher secondary. Sneha is also passionate about spreading positivity and motivational talks. She loves penning poem and quotes. Her dedication is what sets her apart from anybody else. She is well rounded individual who live with passion, dedication and grace.
(Instagram @sneha_kannusamy)

I ADMIRE YOU MY DAD.

I admire your ways
You build me up!
I admire your lessons,
You gave me as defending weapons.
You're the one who made me
To read the world
And gave me the warmth with
Your shoulder against the dry cold.
You pointed me to the great heights,
Amidst the unbearable weights.
One fine day! I'll make you proud,
For the sacrifices you made.
Dad! You are the best
And I love you for everything you do.

SIRISHA SUSARLA

Sirisha is a psychologist by profession, she is very passionate about writing poetry and is a published author. She strongly believes that words are people's best friends and poetry is the relationship between words and the writer. (Instagram @Sirisha_susarla)

SUMMER FELL INTO FALL

I saw you
I went head over heels
In the middle of the autumn
When the seasons crawl,
And just like that summer fell into fall

I can just look at you for hours and hours
Your eyes are something
More beautiful than the stars
You are for me one of all,
And just like that summer fell into fall

Because when you smile,
My heartbeat stops for a while
You are my deepest secret
Shhhh! I have seen an ear in the wall,
And just like that summer fell into fall

You draw my attention when you are in blue
As warm skies draw the exhaling dew
Looking at the way you are
The world seems so small,
And just like that summer fell into fall

SHAKTHI KARUNANIDHI

She is an 18 year old budding pharmD student. Writing is her passion. Her works are so simple and causes the reader to feel the depth in her works. She is a zonal level yoga gold medalist. Her ultimate goal is to achieve big in the writing world. Her genre of writing is vivid. She is good at basketball, badminton, athletics. She is more of a reader than a writer. She is always cheery and positive.
(Instagram @the_phoenix_writer25)

DEAR FATHER!

Father, after hearing this word
The first thing that comes to our mind is
The warming relationship or born shared between
A daughter and her father.

I came out from my mom's womb like all other children,
I was just like the unbloomed flowers of the Linden,
The mixed emotions you had in your eyes,
Was maybe due to the fragments of nostalgia of your mother!
You thought of me as your mom's trice,
The reason for you showing so much love to me,
All actions of the little me was totally silly,
Yet though you are one person who saw goods in it,
Each time you pushed to me to grow my boundaries,
I was just like that unmolded metal in a foundry,
The harsh times, I always wondered, how far you would stay mum,
You usually handle the sad lump,
As though it was a speck of dust,
Got swept in a light blown gust,
I admire you for no reason,
When you overcame all the treason,
With that admirable smile of yours,
Which always made my fears to tear,
I admire your every move as a admirer,
Because you were the one who taught me to see the beauty in my nightmares!
With love,
Your secret admirer!

PRIYADHARSHINI. T

She's Priyadharshini. She is an English literature student, who loves to read and write. She is engrossed in writing poems, short stories, blogs and quotes. She is a budding writer and a movie lover too.
(Instagram @pd28815)

MAN OF MOTIVATION

I was gliding over melancholic thoughts,
My soul was drenched in lassitude,
Silence girdled me,
Solitude embraced me,
I can sense my energy was ebbing away,
My despondency sapped my friskiness,
I cursed myself for being a pinhead,
I was trying to find answers in my seclusion,
But on one fortunate day;
When I was browsing on some videos,
Suddenly a video clip captured my attention,
A clip with a philosophical quote,
I just randomly clicked on to that video,
The clip spanned only for 30 seconds,
But it toppled my entire thought process,
Later I found that prominent saying was framed by a Legend,
His name is 'Bruce Lee'.

Started cumulating each and every attributes of him,
I completely scrutinized about him,
I was just stunned, how come a man can lead such an esteemed life,
Commenced reading his highly acclaimed biography,
Gradually I started to go crazy for him,
I got so very pensive about his philosophies,
It's his sayings which instigated me to hanker my goal,
He dynamited my inner-self,
He glistened my mind with sanguine sparkles,
He brought out the perky version of me,
It's he who nurtured optimistic seeds within me,
He who taught me to mutate my pain into positive energy,

He who quashed my disheartened ruminations,
He who gave me positive vibes,
He who transformed me into a strong soul,
My home walls are embellished with his sayings,
Whenever I see it, my eyes just scintillates with cheery glitters,
His golden words set my heart on fire to attain my aspiration,
I am proud to follow his pearls of wisdom,
But! Why he's so famous?
Ostensibly the answer is quite very simple;
He's the Man of Self-confidence,
He's the Man of Motivation,
His name became a byword for 'Kung Fu',
An actor, director, dancer, philosopher;
An astounding Martial artist, what not?
A gentle and a self-effacing soul!

He inscribed his name in the pages of history with his persistent diligence and assiduity,
He imprinted his footsteps stronger than anyone could do,
There may be many kings in the world of Martial arts,
But, he's the God of Martial arts.
He's my Demigod; he's my idol,
He's my inspiration; he's my role model,
He's my teacher; he's my super hero,
Of course he's the person, I admire.

ADHITHYA

She's a writer, who pens whenever she wishes to make a wish for admiring the beauty of writing through her words! (Instagram @its_the_special_edition)

HER LONGING MATE!

The Blind trust she has,
Was a newer since years!
He who,
Takes up her wishes as his ultimate goals,
Puts her right, when she
Misjudges herself to be,
His cute child he says,
Treasuring hope in her
Saves all his patience,
For tolerating her cute abuses,
Never minds his ease
Caring about her luxury,
Works even in twilight
For securing her euphoria,
For all he gets her,
She's just stealing his first name
And admiring him forever!

TAMILARASI HARIKUMAR. R

She is an English teacher. She loves to teach English. She is excellent in her profession and passion as a writer.

MY ESTEEM DR.KALYANA KUMARI

Her appearance tells that she is an angel.
Her eye sight tells that she is honest.
Her smile tells that she is kind.
Her speech tells that she is bold.
Her face tells that she is lovable.
Her hand tells that she is open- handed.
Her footstep tells that she is patience.
Her dressing tells that she is simple.
Her behaviour tells that she is impartiality.
Her action tells that she is sincere.
Her versatile work tells that she is talented.
Her achievement tells that she is hard-worker and multi-talented person.
Her knowledge tells that she is studious.
Her attitude tells that she is phenomenal.
And because of this, I admire her a lot!

Sr SUJATHA BALASWAMI. N

Sr Sujatha Balaswami is a religious nun in Roman Catholic Church and a writer pursuing her Undergraduate in English literature in Madurai, Tamilnadu, India. She is from Kurnool in Andhra Pradesh. She is a co-author of two Anthologies. She is a writer by passion and a literarian by profession. Her goal is to inspire people through her writings and form positivity everywhere.
(Instagram @Suja)

I ADMIRE THY

Father who raised me with lots of loveliness
Father who held me with lots of tenderness
Father who helped me to live freely
Father who loved me unconditionally

I always admire you for you are my life giver
I always admire you for you are my protector
I always admire you for you are so kind hearted
I always admire you for you are my best friend

You are the man of god who purely loves
You are the generous hearted who helps always
You are the hard worker who works for my happiness
Your Godly life has made me to live my life in fullness

Thank you for teaching me everything with gentleness
You are my role model, my hero and love you always

DIOTIMA BOSE

Diotima Bose is pursuing her Masters in Chemistry from Chandigarh University. She is a student of classical music, a disciple of Padmabhushan Pandit Ajoy Chakraborty. Writing has always been her passion. One of her poems has been selected for World Record Attempt and for being published in a Poetry Anthology Book. She has successfully completed her Creative Writing workshop from the organization My Captain, one of the best 50 worldwide platforms. Diotima has also recently co-authored in a book. She is even enlisted as an aspiring writer on various online websites and platforms of social media.
(Instagram @Diotima Bose)

THE LIGHT OF MY LIFE

The woman who made me see the first ray of the sun,
She who let me give out my first cry,
The one who knew my senses better than me,
Is of course the person I admire.

A mother's love is inexplicable, unfathomable as we know,
No different is her maternal love, unique as it is;
She is my Sun who lends light me light,
She is my Moon who sinks down for me to rise!

A distinct figure as she is in person
Filled with love, care and affection,
A strict teacher resides in her
Full of hope, courage and passion.

Studies, music, stitching, cooking,
And so much so in her genes
Render her a distinct innate glow from within
Making her an ideal human being.

The voice she has been endowed with
Is no less than that of a Nightingale,
The heart she carries within herself
Is more than one can even imagine.

Its not because of My Mother I admire,
Its because of her virtues that all do;
Its not just because she has given me life,
Its also because she makes me who I am.

Days, nights, dusk, dawn,

Summers, winters, rains and autumns,
She is the woman making me heal
Taking me out from life's sorrowful reel.

'Mother' as it says by name
Is much more than just a poem,
She means more than the word itself
Just as My Mother is the world's best-self!

SHRUTI AGARWAL

Shruti agarwal, 23, is residing Rajasthan, India with her family. She has completed her graduation and now she is pursuing the chartered accountancy course (CA) under respected institute of chartered accountant of India (ICAI).Her inspiration is her mother .She loves to express her feelings through writing inspirational quotes, love poems, heart breaking poems and through drawing and singing . She believes in "don't stop shining just because someone gets inspired by your light.
(Instagram @Shaan_0612)

A BELIEVE OF THEIST

A curved trunk, elephant headed boy surrounds me all the time,
I am not able to see him from my eyes,
But my heart always feels him!
A cute little, heavenly Angel flies in my life,
I am not able to go to him,
But he comes to me to protect me!
In my life dreams he comes to me,
Wraps me in his trunk,
Brings me into the heavens, he flies off to the universe,
Later, he brings me back to that place
Where everything is transformly settled,
Where no obstacles are there for me
And the path is clear for a new beginning!
Whether it is my dream or reality of my life,
Hey Ganesha! You don't say anything to me,
But I can say that you are working in my life!
Guiding me,
Protecting me,
And loving me all the time!

KAYAL. R

Kayal. R is pursuing her UG final year in PSG college of Arts and Science. She is a young budding writer. She is not a famous poet or writer, yet she wishing to be one. She is the one who loves to explore the beauty of writing. (Instagram @kayalraju_571)

REGARDS TO ORIGINATES

I'm wishing not much in abode,
Trying to explore new.
Why do my wish turned your dreams,
Thy sacrifice for my best,
I Have been blessed with your
Support and strength
You may see me struggle,
But you never let me fail.
You may get hurt by my misconstrue,
But you still construct me, by thy virtue.
You embrace Me
By your unconditional love.
I'm so much of what,
I learned from you.
It is neither wealth nor splendour,
But tranquillity and occupation,
Which gives us happiness.
You always been my felicity and delicacy.
I don't think you can go wrong,
Where is love and inspiration.
If I go to whilom,
I will bless you with all blessings, that I ever had
My dear originates, you are the artworks that I could
admire forever.

RUPA BHARTI

This is Rupa Bharti who is belonging from Bihar, who is pursuing MBA from Sinhgad institute Pune, from finance and marketing department. She is a co-author, an artist, poet and writer, she wants to brings some facts of society and she wants to motivate the people through her poem and story. she always try to observe the little thing whatever is going her surrounding and she always try to explain the things through her poem, story and art she live her life with the inspirations and she is a dreamer, Rupa is just not complete within herself she is completely strong with her feelings. Now she came with her own thoughts.
(Instagram @rupabharti1210@)

ONE DAY

One day, when you will be success
Everyone will admire you,
Everyone will start to follow you.

One day, when you will do good for someone,
That person will admire you,
That person will hope you.

While you will do for the nature,
Nature will admire you,
Nature will expect you.
Basically, it's the rule of nature.

It is the rule of nature
Because, there is no one above the nature,
All are bounded by the thread of nature,
Here all are the human being.

One day, if you will love someone,
Might be that person will always admire you,
There is no other single person who always admire you without any desire,
The person will admire you,
According to your passion for the work.

Now-a-days, we are getting so busy in observing that
Whether they admire me or they didn't.
Some days we have to pressurize the people,
For admiring me, And it's a human tendency.

KIRUBAVATHI VISVARAJ. S

An engineering graduate worked as teacher being a mom of two year kid
(Instagram @jayam.kiruba)

THE LEADER

A mentor is she to many
The best tutor she's been
An unbeatable orator being exemplified by all
A kindler of many creative minds
Her astonishing attires grab our attention
Working under her leaves us in no tension
Unbiased natured principal who
Gets mingled with her followers as their pal
The most gorgeous is she
Eye catchy calligraphy that she owns
Her love for others is as soft as breeze
Her support to us is as much as uncontrollable water fall
Her anger is like the mist
Her majestic walk is more enough to be an inspiring leader
Mother, Friend, Teacher, Principal our well dignified leader
Whose motherly care attracts everyone as magnet
The person I admire is my principal who taught me 'how to be many!'

LOHITHA DEVI MADDIPOTI

She is the one who believes in herself and drives herself through her passion.
(Instagram @passion_phactory)

MY DEAR GRANDPA

My Childhood was so beautiful,
It's because of you,
It's all because of you I miss you
The way you used to hold me,
The lessons you taught me,
The morals you have given me,
The memories you gave me,
The outings we used to have,
The funny conversations of us,
The food we used to share,
The fun we used to have,
Everything seemed so beautiful
I still remember the day,
When I saw you last time before
You left me forever
My eyes filled with tears,
My mouth didn't utter a word,
My hands were shivering,
My heart was crying for you
I cried whole night sitting in the balcony,
But now I'm surviving with the hope that,
You are with me in everything to guide and take care of me
I miss you Grandpa, I miss you
Though you are not with me,
My admiration for you never fades.

BHAVIKA DHIRAJ SINDHI

Bhavika Dhiraj Sindhi a 25 year old creative writer. She belongs to Turkey an Indian writing from abroad due to her passion in writing. She is a curious girl, a wanderer who likes to explore new things and places. She is a hard-headed but soft-hearted person. She uses her pen as her best friend to speak her feelings. Believes only love can make this place a better to survive..!
(Instagram @she_is_troublesome)

WITHERED ROSE

A person who gave me life lessons held me up.
But when the time when God wanted to test her teachings he took her away!
So that they could see me together.
The moon and the star shining feels like them
At times when I'm low, she breaks herself so that I can wish and she will fulfil it
To my mom in heaven
So that is I miss you so much
My words are less to describe you
The warmth of your arms
Your lap!
I wish I just could sleep once
To the great human being who made me
To the one who always looked as a star in me
To the one who loved me with selfless thought
I couldn't find any soul on this earth like you.
To the irreplaceable human of my life
The oxygen to my life you were
I still remember how hard you struggled to survive
The sunshine to my darkness
You went and it was so dark again
I shined from your light
I felt you always holding my back

They thought it was easy though
Broken mentally and emotionally!
Yet your words are still in my ears
You are my brave baby
Let's win the world
There's a rose in my value education book of 5th std

To one which my mom gifted me From her garden To the one she always took care just as me
I still have preserved
For she use to tell me the fairy tales
That some prince will come and take me
To the smell is it still fresh
Just like in my memories
From the heaven shall be watching me
I just would say Thank you mom
For the person you being
To the values you added to my life
To holding hands
And teaching me
The food you made
As all the fragrance in my brain
To just once I wish to hug you back
The day I miss you more I just open that book and
Just smell that rose
Among the selfish people, I just miss your selfless love
Those head massage
And stories at the night
My life saviour you would be
To the rose of my life
The thorns hurt me
Just like the fragrance I have lost
The essence of my life
To the love u gave was irreplaceable mom
To the heaven would cherish to have a angel like you
I didn't realise till the fragrance was gone
Dad says just look she is the shining star
And I want to hold you
Love you, Hug you
And just want that moment forever!

UMA RAJMOHAN

She is an inspiring teacher by profession and one who does it with passion. She can strike a bond instantaneously and nonchalantly. She is an articulate and hyper expressive personality who would like to give back to society what it had given her. She is an amicable individual who is proud to be her-self. One who loved species just as she loved her-self.
(Instagram @uma_rajmohan)

GORGEOUS BLESSED STINT

I admire.
The Lady
The Mom to be
The Altruistic philanthropist
She may perhaps be an outright insurgent.
A notorious brat
But the instant, she recognizes that.
An embryo has implanted,
Itself in the uterine fence
And she has missed her chums.
Her wrist pulsates two different heart beats.
She channelizes her regime.
She gives up her much-loved junk delicacies.
She sets off relishing healthy natural food.
She basks in all the pampering all around
But never crosses the Lakshman Rekha
And aspires to eat, or revel in small little mischief.
She turns into a calm little saint.
Who gathers herself, revels and experiences!
All the three trimesters relentlessly
As much as the glow she got on your cheeks and eyes.
She could not stand or sit without puffing and panting.
Advises are aplenty and flows incessantly.
But she relishes the bitter pills and the pounding.
Of the little angel from within
Without much ado and looks forward to the next kick
In fact, she begins tallying it as the days go by.
She does not fit in to her favourite clothes.
But still takes pleasure in seeing her circumference widen.
She is surrounded by plenty to kindle her fears.
With varied petrifying incidents here and there.
With all her heart and soul
She enters labour eager to harbinger the tiny cherub into the realm of goodness.

NEELUKIRAN

Neelukiran is a graduate of BA English literature. She is working as Project manager in Newgen knowledge works. She is open to new opportunities.
(Instagram @Neelukiran04)

A SOLID TROOPER

Clark gable peppery moustache
Struggles and worries safely stashed
Bad scavenger haunting around
Easy life is nowhere bound
Crowds and crowds with wishes standby
Immersed in colours and fortune entice
Flinched - Love and lusts too vaporize
Bewail - Oh! It sucks soul and smile
Balance, balance, the community thrusts
Fooled up and ended all the way trash
Named them sorrows and positioned upright
Customs and cultures out of sight
Ears shuttered,
Scandals shattered
Profanity undressed,
Virtue impressed
Long, long way to go!
Whither planted, bloom and blow!

Flairs and Glairs, a platform by a student for the students. We are esteemed youth struggling to carve out our path for our future and we follow a basic mindset Since everyone is not born with all-round skills. Joining hands with people who are born to execute it with perfection is the best way to evolve. Self-Evolution is the need of the hour but, evolving as a community is what we strive for. The initiative as kickstarted by, Founder- Mr. Shubham Shah with the motive to utilize the skillset and talent of writing has now a team of 10+ people who are actively participating into newer forms of learning and discovering talents among youngsters. We Provide platform and services like Publishing opportunities, Open mics, Workshops, Hands-on training. Operating with Brand Name of Flairs and Glairs (Publication House), we offer the chance of elevating a passionate writer to an esteemed author With Brand name Teekhe Zasbaaat. We bring to you an opportunity to get accustomed with the Public Speaking and Presenting of Thoughts along with regular challenges to brush up your inking spirit. The newest initiative to extend our services we introduced in a new writing Platform- The Glittering Fables and Ink Over Tears.

We Choose to Fly Like A Falcon than to be

a Leg Pulling Crab.

To Know More: Infoline – 7781900870
Mail Us At-
flairsandglairs@gmail.com / info@flairsandglairs.in
Or Visit is at
www.flairsandglairs.com / www.flairsandglairs.in
Social Handles- @flairsandglairs @teekhezasbaaat

www.ingramcontent.com/pod-product-compliance
Ingram Content Group UK Ltd.
Pitfield, Milton Keynes, MK11 3LW, UK
UKHW022003190726
13853UKWH00004B/1703

9 789391 302283